"We're here!" cried Mr. Grizzmeyer. "The boys' camp is down at that end of the lake, and the girls' camp is at the other end."

Brother and Bonnie looked at each other.

"Did you say *boys'* camp and *girls'* camp?" they asked.

The Berenstain Bears at CAMP CRUSH

by Stan & Jan Berenstain

A BIG CHAPTER BOOK™

Random House New York

Library of Congress Cataloging-in-Publication Data
Berenstain, Stan.
The Berenstain Bears at Camp Crush / by Stan and Jan Berenstain.
    p.   cm. — (a Big chapter book)
SUMMARY: When the director of Camp Grizzmeyer tries to keep the boys and girls away from each other, he makes an interesting discovery.
ISBN: 0-679-86028-2 (pbk.) — ISBN 0-679-96028-7 (lib. bdg.)
[1. Camps—Fiction.   2. Bears—Fiction.]   I. Berenstain, Jan.   II. Title.   III. Series: Berenstain, Stan.   Big chapter book.
PZ7.B4483Bemi   1994
[Fic]—dc20   94-15995

Manufactured in the United States of America   10 9 8 7 6

BIG CHAPTER BOOKS is a trademark of Berenstain Enterprises, Inc.

Contents

Mervyn "Bullhorn" Grizzmeyer

Chapter 1
Bullhorn Baits His Hook

At Bear Country School, everyone knew Mervyn "Bullhorn" Grizzmeyer. He was the big, tough school vice principal, gym teacher, and team sports coach. Cubs on the sports teams were used to being yelled at by him when they didn't play hard enough. Some cubs were used to seeing his scowling face behind his desk when they misbehaved and were sent to his office. And all the cubs were used to having gym instructions shouted at them in that booming bullhorn voice of his.

1

But Bullhorn Grizzmeyer was just about the last bear on earth that a cub expected to see at home. That's why Brother and Sister Bear were shocked when Papa answered the tree house door on Saturday afternoon and found Mr. Grizzmeyer at their doorstep.

"What's *he* doing here?" Sister whispered to Brother.

"Beats me," Brother whispered back. "But I hope he doesn't want to come in. If he does, that means something's wrong."

"Mr. Grizzmeyer!" said Papa. "This is quite a surprise. Would you like to come in?"

"Don't mind if I do," said Mr. Grizzmeyer. He came into the living room and plumped himself down on the sofa.

Oh, no! thought the cubs. They tried to think of what they might have done wrong at school lately. Sister couldn't think of anything. Brother couldn't either.

Papa called Mama in and took a seat in his easy chair. "Well, Mr. Grizzmeyer," he said, "what brings you to our humble home?"

Mr. Grizzmeyer seemed to read the cubs' minds. "Don't worry, cubs," he said with a wink. "I'm not here about any school problems. *This* is why I'm here." He took a

brochure from his jacket pocket and unfolded it for the Bears to see.

On the brochure was a picture of a lake with mountains in the background. On the lake were bears in a canoe.

"Here," he said, handing the brochure to Papa. "Have a closer look."

Mama and the cubs gathered around Papa's easy chair.

"Camp Grizzmeyer?" said Papa. "You're the owner of a summer camp?"

"And the director," said Mr. Grizzmeyer. "It's an old Bear Scout campsite on the

scenic slopes of the Great Grizzly Mountains. My wife, Mollie, and I spent our life savings to buy the place. And a wonderful place it is! Just think of it, cubs—the wild beauty of the Great Grizzly Mountains, fishing, swimming, canoeing, softball, basketball, tennis, arts and crafts..."

Camp Grizzmeyer sounded good. But the cubs had never been away from home for more than an overnight, except for the week at Gramps and Gran's when Mama

and Papa had gone on a second honey-moon. A whole summer away from home? It sounded like forever.

"And that's not all," said Mr. Grizzmeyer.

"Every Saturday night we'll have a big dance, complete with disc jockey. And most exciting of all are the All-Camp Games that will finish up the summer. All four area camps will meet just down the mountain at Camp Sunshine. Along with the usual sports, a musical show will be part of the competition. I'll bet you cubs won't want to miss the biggest event of the summer!"

Brother and Sister were more interested now. "How many cubs will be there?" asked Sister.

"Lots," said Mr. Grizzmeyer. "About half of them are from Bear Country School, and the other half from Big Bear City School. I expect most of your friends to sign up: Lizzy and Barry Bruin, Cousin Fred, Ferdy Factual. A few already have: Babs Bruno, Queenie McBear..." He paused and glanced at Brother. "Oh, yes...and Bonnie Brown," he added. "Better make up your minds quickly, cubs. There's only a week of school left, and Camp Grizzmeyer will be full before you know it."

Papa told him that the Bear family would talk it over and give him their decision soon. Mr. Grizzmeyer thanked them and left.

"Well, it sure sounds fun to me," Papa told the cubs. "What do you think?"

Brother turned it over in his mind. He had never before thought of spending a whole summer with Mr. Grizzmeyer. On the other hand, he had never thought of spending a whole summer *without* Bonnie Brown. And that was exactly what would happen if Bonnie went to Camp Grizzmeyer and he didn't.

"The All-Camp Games sound great," Brother said at last. "Count me in."

Sister was two years younger than Brother, and Mama was wondering if she was ready to spend a summer away from home. Sister was wondering the same thing.

"Come on, Sis," said Brother. "It'll be great. You'll wow everybody at those Saturday night dances. And it isn't as if you'll be all alone. We'll be together."

That was enough to convince Sister. "Okay, I'll do it," she said.

"Fine," said Papa. "I'll call Mollie Grizzmeyer right away while there's still room on the sign-up sheet."

Chapter 2
Too-Tall's Problem

On Monday morning, as they waited in the schoolyard for the school bell to ring, Brother and Sister talked about Camp Grizzmeyer with some of their friends. Cousin Fred had learned that Brother and

Sister weren't the only cubs who had signed up over the weekend. Several others, including Bertha Broom and Gil Grizzwold, had also decided to go to the new summer camp. As the cubs talked in excited voices, Too-Tall Grizzly and his gang pushed up against them.

"Excuse me, cubs," said Too-Tall sweetly. "I couldn't help overhearing your conversation."

"And?" said Brother.

"And I think you're all nuts!" said Too-Tall.

"All right, big shot," said Brother. "Why are we all nuts?"

"Because you're gonna spend all summer with Mr. Grizzmeyer," said Too-Tall. "That's not what summer means to me and the gang. Go ahead, Skuzz. Tell 'em what summer means to us."

Skuzz cleared his throat and said:

"No more pencils! No more books!
No more Grizzmeyer's dirty looks!"

"The idea of summer," said Too-Tall, "is not to hang around with Mr. Grizzmeyer. The idea is to get *away* from Mr. Grizzmeyer."

"Gee, Too-Tall," said Sister. "When I heard about Queenie signing up for Camp Grizzmeyer, I thought you'd be all hot to go too."

"Queenie?" said Too-Tall. He sounded surprised.

"Sure," teased Barry Bruin. "You'd better sign up while there's still time..."

"Shut up!" barked Too-Tall. "Shut up before you get *beat* up!" He grinned wickedly. "Sure, I may miss Queenie a little. But I'm gonna miss the rest of you a *lot*."

"You are?" said Sister.

"Why's that?" asked Brother.

"Because we won't have anybody to beat up all summer!" said Too-Tall. "Right, gang?"

"Right, Chief," said Skuzz.

"Yeah," added Smirk. "It'll be terrible. We may have to beat up *each other!*"

Too-Tall and the gang began dancing around like boxers, laughing as they slapped at each other.

"Creeps!" said Fred as he and Brother

headed for class. Then he turned to Brother and said, "Do you think Too-Tall will change his mind and sign up for camp? He's really hooked on Queenie."

"Nope," said Brother. "And that's fine with me. Too-Tall will be really glad to get away from Mr. Grizzmeyer, and that's just how glad *I'll* be to get away from him and his gang."

Chapter 3
A-Camping We Will Go!

The following Saturday, the campers and their parents gathered in front of Bear Country School to wait for the bus that would take them to Camp Grizzmeyer. Too-Tall Grizzly was nowhere to be seen. It seemed that Brother had been right about him.

"Hey, Queenie," said Babs Bruno. "Where's your boyfriend? Isn't he even going to kiss you good-bye?"

"He's mad at me," said Queenie. "You know how he is when things don't go his way."

Just then an old school bus rolled over the hill and into view. Mr. Grizzmeyer was at the wheel.

"Looks kind of old and creaky," said Brother to Bonnie Brown.

"Maybe that's why we're supposed to travel light," said Bonnie.

Mr. Grizzmeyer had told the campers to bring just one item other than clothing and the items on the camp list. Brother had brought his baseball glove. Sister had brought her teddy bear. Fred had brought his dictionary. And Queenie had brought her tape deck and rock-'n'-roll tapes.

Right behind Mr. Grizzmeyer sat Mrs. Grizzmeyer. The front half of the bus was already filled with campers from Big Bear City.

Mr. Grizzmeyer waved cheerfully as he

hopped down from the bus. "All right, folks," he said. "Finish your good-byes, and let's get going."

Mrs. Grizzmeyer got off the bus too. She talked to the cubs and parents. Some of the younger cubs, including Sister, were still a little nervous about going to overnight camp. It helped that Mrs. Grizzmeyer was as friendly and nice as her husband was loud and gruff.

The cubs said good-bye to their parents and boarded the bus. Mr. Grizzmeyer shifted into gear, and they were on their way.

As the old bus picked up speed on the flat stretch of road outside of town, the campers could feel the excitement in the air. When Mr. Grizzmeyer struck up a jolly song, they were all more than willing to join in.

"A-camping we will go!
A-camping we will go!
Hi, ho, the merry-o!
A-camping we will go!"

As they headed for the foothills of the
Great Grizzly Mountains, the cubs began to
chat with one another. Brother and Bonnie,
who were delighted to be spending the
summer together, talked happily. But
Queenie, sitting with Babs Bruno, didn't
look at all happy.

"Why the long face?" asked Babs.

"Too-Tall," said Queenie.

"But just a few minutes ago, you were laughing about his being mad at you," said Babs.

"I know," said Queenie. "But now I feel sad. I already miss the big lug!"

As Babs tried to cheer Queenie up, Ferdy Factual talked with Trudy Brunowitz in the next seat. Trudy had moved to town with her family only a week before. None of the cubs knew anything about her. She had shown up at the bus stop that morning wearing a T-shirt with a famous physics equation printed on it: $E=mc^2$. Of course,

Ferdy had struck up a conversation with her right away. She was short, like Ferdy, and wore thick glasses like Ferdy's. Except for being a girl, she looked a lot like Ferdy. Now the two of them were looking into each other's eyes and talking away as if they were the only ones on the bus.

"I did a science report at Big Bear City School on mesons," said Trudy.

"Mesons?" said Ferdy. "Mesons are of some interest. But they're sort of old news. I'm into quarks myself."

"Actually, my report was on mini-mesons, not ordinary mesons," said Trudy. "They have fascinating interactions with quarks, you know."

"Oh, *mini*-mesons," said Ferdy. "That's different!"

Behind them, Babs asked Queenie, "What language is that, anyway?"

"Nerd-speak," said Queenie.

"Hmm," said Babs, listening. "I think a bit of crush-speak is mixed in with the nerd-speak."

The excitement of going on a great adventure made the time pass quickly. Before they knew it, they were climbing the winding road into the foothills. The old bus wheezed and groaned. The landscape grew wilder. Trees loomed larger and the underbrush got thicker. Soon they rounded a bend...and there it was!

Camp Grizzmeyer!

Chapter 4
Dream Camp

Nestled among the foothills, the camp rested on the shore of a beautiful blue lake. There were a dozen cabins and a big administration building made of huge logs. There was a rec hall, well-kept athletic fields, and a full-size swimming course laid out at the edge of the lake.

What a sight! What a setup! What a place to spend the summer!

The bus rolled right up to the camp entrance...*and past it!*

"Stop!" shouted the cubs. "Wait!" "Whoa!"

"Hey!" cried Bertha Broom. "Why aren't we stopping?"

"No reason to," said Mr. Grizzmeyer. "This isn't Camp Grizzmeyer. This is Camp Sunshine." He glanced over his shoulder to see the cubs staring out their windows in shock and disappointment as the lovely campgrounds grew smaller and smaller in the distance. "Camp Softy, they ought to call it," he growled. "You might as well stay home as go to a sissy place like Camp Sunshine. Grizzmeyer campers are tough! And we'll prove it later when we come back here and beat these Sunshine softies in every All-Camp event!"

The bus creaked on into the mountains.

The air got thinner and thinner. The slopes got steeper and steeper. The road got bumpier and bumpier, until it was hardly a road at all but just a couple of deep ruts.

At last the bus rumbled to a stop. The cubs peered out. There was no sign of anything that looked like a camp. Just mountains, trees, and thick underbrush. They were in the middle of nowhere.

"Maybe the bus broke down," Bonnie said to Brother.

"Or we're out of gas," said Brother. "I hope Mr. G. thought to bring along some extra."

Mr. Grizzmeyer stood up and turned to face the cubs. He didn't seem the least bit worried about the bus stopping. In fact, he was beaming. "Everyone out of the bus!" he cried. "We're here!"

No one moved.

Brother and Bonnie looked at each other and shrugged. Ferdy Factual gave Trudy Brunowitz a puzzled look.

"Mr. Grizzmeyer," said Ferdy. "It looks to me as if we're in the middle of nowhere."

"Precisely, Ferdy, my boy," said Mr. Grizzmeyer. "And what better place could you choose for a true wilderness experience?"

"Wilderness experience?" said Queenie. "I thought we were going to camp."

"Come on," shouted Mr. Grizzmeyer. "It's a bit off the road. We'll have to hike in."

"Hike in?" grumbled Ferdy. "If I'm not mistaken, we were supposed to come to camp to go hiking. Not go hiking to get to camp."

Mr. Grizzmeyer unloaded their gear, and the campers piled off the bus. Mrs.

Grizzmeyer moved among the cubs and spoke quietly as she helped them with their backpacks. "I know you're all tired," she said. "But it's just a little bit farther." She gave each of the smaller cubs a hug or a squeeze.

"It's a good thing *Mrs.* G. is along," said Bonnie.

"You've got *that* right," said Brother.

"All set?" shouted Mr. G.

"All set!" answered Mrs. G.

"Then let's go-o-o!" bellowed. Mr. G. He drew a big machete from a sheath on his backpack and started hacking his way through the underbrush. Over his shoulder he yelled, "Bring up the rear, if you will, Mrs. G.! We don't want to lose any campers on the very first day!"

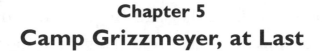

LET'S GO-O-O!

Chapter 5
Camp Grizzmeyer, at Last

The hike to Camp Grizzmeyer was only a few hundred yards. But it seemed like miles. Grunting and groaning, the cubs lugged their suitcases and heavy backpacks through thornbushes and over fallen trees. When at last they reached a clearing at the edge of a small lake, Mr. Grizzmeyer was the only one smiling. "Here it is!" he cried. "Isn't it magnificent!"

But the campers didn't answer. They were too busy scratching their insect bites and picking thorns from their clothing.

Finally, Babs Bruno looked around and said, "The little lake is nice, Mr. G. But where are the cabins?"

Mr. Grizzmeyer pointed to the woods on his left. "The boys' camp is down at that end of the lake," he said. He pointed to the woods on his right. "And the girls' camp is at the other end."

ISN'T IT MAGNIFICENT!

Brother and Bonnie looked at each other. Ferdy and Trudy looked at each other. Queenie, who had already forgotten all about Too-Tall, looked around at all the boys from Big Bear City. Then she looked up at Mr. Grizzmeyer. "Did you say *boys'* camp and *girls'* camp?" she asked.

"That's right," said Mr. Grizzmeyer. He

raised his whistle to his lips and blew a long shrill blast. "Counselors, come take charge of your campers!" he shouted.

From the woods came bears wearing T-shirts with names printed on them. Some of the bears were teenagers. Others seemed older. All the counselors coming from the

left were male, and all those coming from the right were female.

"It's true!" Brother whispered to Bonnie. "We're going to be in *separate camps!*"

Sister tugged at Brother's sleeve. "I'm scared," she whined. "I wanna be with *you.*"

"Sorry, Sis," said Brother. Then he noticed a big friendly-looking counselor heading toward the Bear Country School campers. His T-shirt said "Counselor Mike" on it. Before he reached the campers, he turned and went over to the group of female counselors. He began whispering to a pretty counselor whose T-shirt said "Counselor Margie."

When he saw this, Mr. Grizzmeyer blew his whistle again and roared, "I *said* take charge of your campers!"

Counselor Mike stopped talking to Margie and came over to the cubs. He

looked down at his clipboard and read, "Brother Bear, Cousin Fred, Barry Bruin, Ferdy Factual, Gil Grizzwold. You're all in my cabin. Follow me."

"Counselor?" asked Brother.

"Call me Mike, son," said the counselor.

"I'm worried about my little sister," said Brother. "I sort of look out for her. We didn't know we'd be at separate camps."

Counselor Mike checked his clipboard. "She's in Counselor Margie's cabin. Margie's great with little cubs. Your sister will be fine. Besides, you'll see her at meals every day. Both camps share the mess hall. And there are the Saturday night dances."

Counselor Mike seemed like a pretty good guy. Maybe he was right about Sister. She was a tough little cub. Maybe it would do her good to be on her own. But Brother couldn't see what good it would do him to be separated from Bonnie all summer. They'd made plans. Bonnie was going to help him with his tennis game, and he was going to teach Bonnie how to swim. Because of her busy schedule—Bonnie was a model and also did some acting on TV— she had never learned to swim. Brother wanted to ask the counselor why the boys were separated from the girls. But he was too embarrassed.

Chapter 6
Call This Place a Camp?

Counselor Mike led his group along a muddy road to the boys' camp. As they walked, the cubs got more and more discouraged. Up ahead were some very run-down buildings. Workers were fixing them up.

"This is the main camp," said Mike. "That long building is the mess hall."

"It sure is a mess," said Ferdy.

IT SURE IS A MESS.

"That big building is the rec hall," said the counselor.

"It certainly is a wreck," said Ferdy.

"And that small building is the infirmary," said Mike.

"It certainly does look infirm," said Ferdy.

As they moved on, some of the other cubs began to grumble.

"Filthy rotten cheat," said Barry.

"Call this place a camp?" said Cousin Fred.

"Calling this place a camp," said Ferdy, "is like calling a baloney sandwich a full-course turkey dinner with all the trimmings. Calling this place a camp is like calling...like calling..." Words didn't fail super-smart Ferdy very often. But Camp Grizzmeyer was proving too much even for Ferdy's fertile brain.

"Like calling this muddy road a four-lane superhighway?" said Counselor Mike with a smile.

It seemed to Brother that the big counselor really was a good guy. He could have

come down hard on Ferdy and the other complainers. Instead, he let them have their say.

"Okay, fellows," said Mike. "This is the boys' camp, and there's your cabin."

The boys' camp was really just a place where the muddy road dribbled out. And the cabin was not much more than an open-air platform with a roof over it and a sign that said CABIN 1.

"Calling this a cabin," said Ferdy, "is like..."

"That'll be enough," said the counselor. "It's time to stop complaining and get to work. This is going to be our home for the summer. Let's make the best of it."

Chapter 7
Giving Camp a Chance

Brother agreed with Mike. It wasn't going to do any good to keep complaining. Besides, the cabin seemed different inside—that is, if an open-air cabin *has* an inside. It wasn't exactly cozy. But it had a terrific view of the lake on one side and the forest on the other.

"Are you with us, Brother?" said Mike. He handed Brother a broom.

"Huh?" said Brother. All the others had brooms and were hard at work sweeping out last year's leaves. Except for Barry.

"You're not sweeping, Barry," said Mike.

"I'm writing a letter," said Barry. "You can read it if you want." He handed it to Mike.

This is what the letter said:

Dear Mom and Dad,
This place is a dissaster!
It's the pits!
It's a filthy rotten cheat!
Come and get me NOW!!!
Your loving son
Barry

"You've got too many *s*'s in 'disaster,'" said Mike.

"Thanks," said Barry. "I'll fix it."

Mike called the other cubs over. "I know

you're all pretty disappointed in the camp so far," he said. "It's not the most modern camp around. And it doesn't have lots of equipment. But the Grizzmeyers have sunk their life savings into it. They've got crews working around the clock to fix it up."

A cloud of gnats couldn't have picked a worse time to swarm into the cabin. "GNATS!" screamed the cubs, swatting wildly. Mike pulled a can of bug spray from his backpack and got rid of the gnats with a few poofs.

"Anybody got a stamp?" yelled Barry.

"Barry's got a point, Mike," said Brother.

"The bugs'll eat us alive in this place."

"No, they won't," said Mike. "The mosquito nets will protect you tonight. And by tomorrow the cabins will be screened in. The girls' cabins are already screened in."

Brother was glad to hear that. Sister was bad about mosquito bites. She just wouldn't stop scratching. Thinking about Sister got him thinking about Bonnie again.

"So we're making progress," said Mike. "Try to give camp a few more days."

Barry agreed not to send his letter. At least, not yet. Brother was trying to get up the courage to ask Mike why the boys and girls were separated. But Ferdy beat him to it.

"Do you want the short answer or the long answer?" said Mike.

"Both," said Ferdy.

"The short answer is that this place was

45

originally a Bear Scout camp. It was divided into a boys' camp and a girls' camp when Mr. G. bought it. So he decided to keep it that way."

"What's the long answer?" asked Brother.

"The long answer," said Mike, beginning to get a little hot under the collar as he spoke, "is that Mr. G. is a mean, stubborn, narrow-minded old coot who thinks boys and girls can't be trusted. He thinks that if you don't keep them separated, they'll all get crazy crushes on each other and give the camp a bad name!"

"Gee, I don't buy that," said Brother. "If that were true, how could we all go to school together and learn anything. I was looking forward to swimming and canoeing and playing tennis with Bonnie Brown this summer."

Ferdy said, "And *I* was looking forward to

further scientific discussions with my new friend, Trudy Brunowitz."

"*You* don't buy it? *You* don't buy it?" Big Mike was really hot under the collar now. "Counselor Margie and I are *engaged!* And the old coot knows it! We hardly get to see each other! You saw how he gave me the whistle when I tried to talk to her." Mike sighed. "But, hey, I shouldn't be dumping my troubles on you guys."

Maybe not, thought Brother. But he felt a little better knowing that he and his counselor were in the same boat.

"Camp Grizzmeyer," sneered Ferdy.

"They ought to call it Camp *Quag*mire."

"Quagmire?" said Barry.

"Quagmire," said Cousin Fred. "An area of sloppy, boggy ground where it is easy to get stuck."

"And, boy, are we stuck!" said Brother.

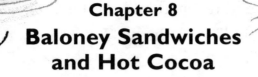

Chapter 8
Baloney Sandwiches and Hot Cocoa

Once the cabin was cleaned up, the cubs stretched out on their cots. They were angry, tired, disgusted...and HUNGRY.

"Hey, Counselor," said Ferdy. "Don't we get to eat at Camp Quagmire?"

"Sure," said Mike. "Here comes the supper cart now."

"Huh?" said Brother. "Aren't we going down to the mess hall?" He was eager to touch base with Sister...*and* Bonnie.

"Mess hall won't be ready until tomorrow's breakfast," said Mike.

The supper cart was a big tricycle with a box in front. Counselor Max, who was pedaling, handed Mike a big brown bag and pedaled on. Mike pulled all the cots into a circle and reached into the bag.

"Mmm!" said Barry. "I'm hungry enough to eat a..."

"Baloney sandwich?" said Mike, holding one up high. There were lots and lots of baloney sandwiches. For drinks there were two big thermoses of hot cocoa. The cubs started eating. The stack of baloney sandwiches got smaller and smaller.

"You know something, Ferdy?" said Brother. "If you're hungry enough, baloney sandwiches are *better* than a turkey dinner with all the trimmings."

Chapter 9
The Schedule of the Day

"Hey, Sis," said Brother. "How'd you make out down at the girls' camp?" The cubs from both camps stood in front of the mess hall. They were ready to go in for breakfast.

"Okay, I guess," said Sister. "Counselor Margie is real nice, and I only got one mosquito bite."

"Have you seen Bonnie?"

"Right behind you," said Bonnie. "Don't worry about Sister. She's doing fine."

"Not as fine as Queenie," said Cousin Fred.

Queenie was cozying up to a big cub from Big Bear City. Hmm, thought Brother. Maybe Mr. Grizzmeyer had a point. Maybe some cubs did go crush-crazy at summer

camp. There was a blast on a whistle, and Bullhorn himself bulled his way into the crowd.

"Two lines! Two lines!" he roared. "Boys' line here! Girls' line there!"

The boys and girls stayed separated in the mess hall—boys on one side, girls on the other. Breakfast was simple but good. There

was hot and cold cereal, wild raspberries, milk, and sweet rolls. At exactly 8:30, Mr. Grizzmeyer blew another blast on his whistle and announced the day's schedule.

"8:45: boys' Cabin One: Basketball; girls' Cabin One: Tennis; boys' Cabin Two: Water Safety; girls' Cabin Two..."

Brother and Bonnie looked at each other across the mess hall and shrugged.

Chapter 10
Pitching In

"Look at those weeds!" said Barry. Mike's group was looking at an old blacktop basketball court with hundreds of tall weeds growing up through hundreds of cracks.

"*Daucus carota,*" said Ferdy Factual. "Popularly known as Queen Anne's lace. A very tough and persistent weed."

Counselor Mike looked very disappointed. "The work crews were supposed to have cleared it by now," he said. "Gang, we've got two choices. We can sit around feeling sorry for ourselves, *or* WE CAN START PULLING WEEDS!"

"You heard him, guys," said Brother. "Start pulling!"

Not far away, at the tennis court, Margie's group was looking at a different sort of problem. There was such a big hump in the middle of the court that the net couldn't be strung properly.

"Maybe we could play without a net," said Babs.

"Playing tennis without a net," said Trudy Brunowitz, "is like writing poetry without rhymes."

"Hey, look," said Sister. "Here are some hoes and shovels the work crew must have left."

"We have two choices," said Margie. "We can sit around feeling sorry for ourselves, *or* WE CAN START SCRAPING!"

"You heard the counselor," said Sister. "Start scraping!"

The same kind of thing was happening all over camp. As a result, Camp Grizzmeyer began to look the way a camp is supposed to. Counselor Max's group fixed up the softball field. Counselor Linda's group cleaned up the beaches. Counselor Herb's group pulled the rocks out of the volleyball area.

And all the cabins helped out in the mess hall.

True, it wasn't Camp Sunshine and never would be. But things were improving. All the cabins were screened in. The meals were tasty and on time—there was local mountain honey every day and lake trout every other day. But though things were working out in a lot of ways, the cubs still had one really big, really humongous complaint: Mr. Grizzmeyer's strict rule separating the boys and the girls.

Maybe that was why campers and counselors alike were looking forward to the first Saturday night dance with such excitement.

Chapter 11
Mr. Saturday Night

"Hey, cool," said Barry as he walked into the rec hall.

"Hey, way cool," said Queenie.

Mrs. Grizzmeyer and some counselors were putting the finishing touches on the dance decorations. There were cutout musical notes, crepe-paper ribbons, and lots of balloons. Hanging from the ceiling was a big sign that said "LET'S DANCE!"

"Well, *let's!*" said Queenie, going into a little dance. "Where's the tape deck? I brought a few of my tapes."

"Mr. G. is bringing the tape deck," said Mrs. Grizzmeyer. "Here he comes now." Mr. Grizzmeyer came in loaded down with the tape deck, speakers, and a tape case.

"Here, I'll give you a hand, Mr. G.," said Queenie. She took the tape case.

"Help you with those speakers, Mr. G.?" said Barry.

"No thanks, Barry," said Mr. Grizzmeyer. "I'm fine."

They followed him to the stage at the front of the rec hall.

"Hey, Mr. G.," said Queenie. "Your brochure said Saturday night dances with a disc jockey. Who's gonna be the disc jockey?"

"You're looking at him," said Mr. Grizzmeyer.

"You?" said Queenie.

"That's right. Just call me Mr. Saturday Night."

Queenie and Barry were speechless.

JUST CALL ME MR. SATURDAY NIGHT.

"And I've got some really great tapes," added Mr. Grizzmeyer.

When the word spread through the crowd, there was a big groan.

"Gee," said Babs. "The Saturday night dances are the only time the boys and girls get together. And *he's* going to pick the music?"

Brother and Bonnie looked at each other and shrugged.

Back on the stage, Queenie was making Mr. Saturday Night an offer. "Mr. G., here are some of my tapes," she said. "Maybe you can mix them in with your stuff."

"It's nice of you to offer, Queenie," said Mr. G. as he looked through Queenie's tapes. "But these are all rock-'n'-roll, and I don't think..."

"But it's just soft rock," said Queenie. "There's no punk or heavy metal."

"I don't care if it's hard rock, soft rock, punk rock, hunk rock, junk rock, or heavy metal," said Mr. Grizzmeyer. "I'm just not going to permit any rock-'n'-roll at these dances."

There was another groan from the crowd. Barry had checked through Mr. Grizzmeyer's tapes. "What's he got?" asked Queenie as she and Barry left the stage.

"All kinds of weird stuff," said Barry. "Big band, country, show tunes, folk—and even some *waltzes!*"

"Looks like we're going on a long trip down memory lane," said Queenie.

"OKAY!" Mr. Grizzmeyer shouted out. "MR. SATURDAY NIGHT SAYS, 'LET'S DANCE!'"

The first tape was a very old-fashioned big band tune with lots of saxophones. It wasn't exactly the end of the world, but it *was* disappointing. The cubs and counselors had been looking forward to the dance as a chance to really cut loose. And that just wasn't going to happen.

Chapter 12
Talent Is Where You Find It

Though the Saturday night dances were a musical bust, they gave the boys and girls a chance to see one another. Brother and Bonnie sat out most of the dances and compared notes. They figured they would both make the All-Camp Games. Bonnie was a sure thing for the tennis team, and Brother was a "can't miss" on the basketball squad.

But it was becoming clear that Mr. Grizzmeyer's rule of keeping boys and girls apart could really hurt the camp's chances in the Games. The other camps were much bigger than Camp Grizzmeyer. They had many more cubs to choose their teams from. So it was important that Camp Grizzmeyer's teams be based on talent, not on whether

a cub was a boy or a girl.

One day, Brother raised the talent question with Counselor Mike.

"Sure it's a problem," said Mike. "But I don't know what *I'm* supposed to do about it."

"All I want you to do is talk to Mr. Grizzmeyer," said Brother.

"No way," said Mike. "We don't get along. Besides, he'll never put a girl on a boy's team."

"He put one on the school football team, and it was the same girl I've got in mind for our softball team. Did you ever see Bertha Broom's windmill pitch? She's the greatest softball pitcher in Bear Country. And another thing. If he doesn't change his rule about boys and girls, the whole tennis team will be disqualified."

"How so?" asked Mike.

"Because mixed doubles is required, and you can't *have* mixed doubles without boys and girls on the same team."

"Hmm," said Mike. "I won't talk to old Mr. Stiffneck. But I *will* talk to my m—to Mrs. Grizzmeyer."

Chapter 13
Visitors from Another Planet

The next morning, Brother, Fred, and Barry were in Mr. Grizzmeyer's office.

"Boys," said the camp director, "I don't have much time. A group from Camp Sunshine will be here soon to inspect the camp and sign us up for the All-Camp Games. So state your case."

Brother took a deep breath and said pretty much the same thing he had said to Counselor Mike.

"Boys," said Mr. Grizzmeyer, "I want to win the All-Camp Games as much you do. But rules are rules. And they need to be respected."

"Sir," said Brother. "Does that mean your answer is 'no'?"

"You'll have to excuse me," said Mr. Grizzmeyer, looking out the window. "The group from Camp Sunshine is here." He rushed out of the office.

"Well, I guess that's that," said Brother.

As they left the office, they spotted the group from Camp Sunshine. The visitors had just completed the awful hike from the road.

Mr. Grizzmeyer went over and reached

out to shake hands. But the visitors were too busy picking burs and stickers off their snappy outfits to notice. When Mr. G. leaned over to help them pick off the burs, they swatted his hand away. Still trying to be polite, Mr. Grizzmeyer offered to take them on a tour of the camp. Instead of following him, they rudely turned and disappeared back into the underbrush, in the direction of the road.

Mr. Grizzmeyer was furious. "Did you see that? Did you see that?" he snarled. "Bunch of snobs! Creeps! Weirdos from another planet! Boys, there are exceptions to every rule. Tell Bertha Broom to start warming up. And tell your tennis friends they'd better *win* those mixed doubles!" Then he went into his office and slammed the door so hard the building shook.

$E = mc^2$

Chapter 14
It May Be a Quagmire, but It's *Our* Quagmire

By the next morning, word had spread that a group from Camp Sunshine had insulted Camp Grizzmeyer. The insult made everyone in camp more determined than ever to beat the pants off those snooty camps down the mountain.

Mr. Grizzmeyer didn't like bending his rule. But he felt he had improved his softball and tennis teams' chances in the Games. Now he had to work on *his* sport: basketball. He had the beginnings of a team. Brother Bear was a first-rate point guard, and a couple of Big Bear City cubs looked good. But he had to find a big tough center. Without one, his team wouldn't have a chance.

Mrs. Grizzmeyer had a problem on her mind too: the musical show. It seemed to her that separating boys and girls in a musical show was even dumber than separating them on sports teams. And there wasn't much time left to start putting the show together.

But two things happened at breakfast one day that would help the Grizzmeyers solve their problems. First, somebody put fish heads in the cornflakes. Second, Ferdy Factual handed Mrs. Grizzmeyer a complete script for the musical show. He and Trudy had written it during the Saturday night dances.

"E-E-EEK!" screamed Sister. "There's something awful in the cornflakes!"

"It's fish heads," said Babs.

Mr. Grizzmeyer leaped up. "If the camper that did this prank comes forward," he roared, "I might go easy. If the camper does not come forward, I'll smash him like a bug!" Then he hit the table so hard it knocked over the cornflakes and more fish heads came out.

When nobody came forward, Mr. Grizzmeyer stormed out of the mess hall in a fury.

E-E-EEK!

THERE'S SOMETHING AWFUL IN THE CORNFLAKES!

While the mess hall was still buzzing about the prank, Mrs. Grizzmeyer made a decision. If her husband could break the rules, she could too. She announced that show tryouts would start in the rec hall in half an hour. Boys *and* girls would be welcome.

The tryouts got under way and went well. Brother, Bonnie, and the other campers were amazed at Ferdy and Trudy's script.

"I don't know why you're all so surprised," said Ferdy. "It's well established that musical talent and mathematical ability reside in the same portion of the brain."

"Precisely," said Trudy. "There's a good deal of well-founded research on this matter."

Meanwhile, Queenie was at the mike belting out one of the show's songs while Mrs. Grizzmeyer pounded on the piano.

Then, at lunch, a second prank happened. Someone put big round white stones in with the boiled potatoes. When Mr. Grizzmeyer tried to cut one, it jumped off his plate and fell to the floor with a loud KNOCK! Mr. G. didn't jump up this time. He just got red in the face and glared.

Chapter 15
The Prankster Strikes Again—
Big Time!

Brother's group was jogging to the mess hall for breakfast when they saw Mr. Grizzmeyer's striped pajama bottoms flying at the top of the camp flagpole. The prankster had struck again.

A furious Mr. G. was at the foot of the flagpole with some counselors. He was showing them something that looked like a hat. The counselors were trying hard to keep from laughing. Brother's group and the other cubs weren't even trying. They

were doubled over, flopping around on the ground laughing. Even Counselor Mike, who had been in a bad mood lately, was laughing. Finally, Mr. Grizzmeyer dropped the hat and led the counselors into the woods.

"Say," said Queenie, "I'd know that hat

anywhere. It's Too-Tall's!"

Within seconds, Mr. Grizzmeyer and the counselors were dragging Too-Tall and the gang out of the woods.

"I think he was just lonesome with nobody to beat up," said Cousin Fred.

"It's so romantic," said Queenie. "He must have missed me terribly. Hey, Too-Tall! How'd you get here?"

"Bikes!" he called. "We left them in the woods with those other two bikes!"

Other bikes? thought Brother. What other bikes? In spite of himself, Brother was glad to see Too-Tall and the gang. An idea was beginning to form in his mind.

Brother walked over to the office, where Mr. Grizzmeyer had taken the pranksters. He knocked on the door. When Mr. Grizzmeyer stuck his head out, Brother said, "Sir, I just wanted to remind you that you've got a really good basketball center in your office. Not to mention two starting forwards and a shooting guard."

After a long pause, Mr. Grizzmeyer said, "So I do! So I do!"

It didn't take Mr. Grizzmeyer long to figure out how to bring Too-Tall and the gang into camp. He offered them a choice they could hardly refuse. Choice one: they would be turned over to the mountain police for trespassing, theft, and malicious mischief. Choice two: they could accept scholarships to Camp Grizzmeyer for the last few days of the season and play on the camp's basketball team.

Of course, Too-Tall chose the scholarships. Mr. Grizzmeyer called the cubs' parents with the news. Then he assigned Too-Tall and the gang to Cabin 1 so they could be with their "friends."

Chapter 16
Stunning News

A couple of evenings later, Cousin Fred was giving out the day's mail.

"Here's one for you, Barry," he said. "Here's one for Brother. And here's one for...hmm. This one must have gotten in the wrong pile. It should have gone to the office. It's for Mr. Mervyn Grizzmeyer...*Junior?*"

"I'll take it," said Counselor Mike. "It's something I've been expecting."

"Does that mean what I think it means?" gasped Fred.

The big counselor sighed. "Yep. That's what it means. I'm his son."

"Mr. Grizzmeyer's your *dad*?"

"He's my dad. And I'm his son. And Mrs. G. is my mom. Mike's a nickname."

The cubs were stunned. And before they could say anything, Mike hit them with an even bigger stunner.

"This very important piece of mail just happens to be a marriage license," he said, holding it up for them to see. "Margie and I

LICENSE
FOR
THE MARRIAGE
OF
Mervyn Grizzmeyer Jr.
and
Margaret Bearwood

BEAR
COUNTRY

Wilma Ursula
Clerk of
Bear Coun...

are going to get married tonight. It's all arranged with the local justice of the peace. Those two other bikes Too-Tall mentioned are Margie's and mine."

"Mike, you're grown and I'm just a cub," said Brother. "But are you sure you're doing the right thing?"

"I feel really bad about my mom," said Mike. "I've left her a note. As for my dad, I love him and I'm sure he loves me. But he's dead set against Margie and me getting married. Says we're too young, too immature. But, hey, enough said. As soon as it's a little darker, I'm outta here, and Margie and I are on our bikes and down the mountain to that little old justice of the peace."

"But the All-Camp Games start tomorrow," said Brother. "And what about bed check? It could be your dad checking tonight."

"I'm sorry to be missing the All-Camp Games," said Mike. "But you'll do fine. As for bed check..." He shined his flashlight on his cot, and...*there was somebody in it!* "It's a bed dummy," he said. "Made of straw and stuff."

"But what if Mr. G. does bed check and isn't fooled?" said Cousin Fred.

"Hey, relax," said Mike. "There's no way he can blame you. Dad's tough, but he's not unfair. Look, it's been great knowing you guys. So wish me luck."

The big counselor slipped his backpack on and went out into the night.

"Good luck...," said the cubs. But Counselor Mike had already disappeared into the darkness.

What Brother and the others feared most was exactly what happened. Mr. Grizzmeyer *did* do bed check that night, and he *did* catch on to the bed dummy. He might not have, except for some straw poking through the blanket. When he pulled back the covers and shined his flashlight on the bundle of straw and leaves, the cubs pretended even harder that they were sleeping. But instead of exploding with anger, Mike's father sat on the edge of his son's bed for a while. Then he left and walked slowly back down the road without even checking the other boys' cabins.

Chapter 17
Hitchhikers

By the next morning, word had spread that Mike and Margie had run off and gotten married. For most of the camp it was big news—for about ten minutes. That was because the *really* big news was the All-Camp Games. It wasn't like that for the cubs from Bear Country School who were in Mike's and Margie's cabins. And, of course, it wasn't like that for Mr. and Mrs. Grizzmeyer. Mr. Grizzmeyer was more sad and shaken than angry. Mrs. Grizzmeyer was more worried about Mr. G. than about Mike and Margie. Sure, she would have liked a big Bear Country wedding. But you can't have everything. After all, she and Mr. Grizzmeyer had married young. Their marriage had worked out fine.

But for most of the campers and counselors, the big news and excitement were about the All-Camp Games. And the old bus was part of that excitement. It had a bright new coat of yellow paint. In big letters on its side, it said "GRIZZMEYER— CAMP OF WINNERS!"

"Okay, gang!" shouted Counselor Max. "We'll show those Sunshiners and those other snooty camps! Into the bus!"

Brother and Bonnie sat near the front of the bus, just behind Mrs. Grizzmeyer. Mr. Grizzmeyer was the driver.

"Look!" shouted Brother as the bus rumbled down the mountain road. "Hitchhikers!"

Just down the road were two hitchhikers

standing at the side of the road—*and they had bikes!*

"Stop the bus!" shouted Mrs. Grizzmeyer. "It's Mike and Margie!"

"Well, I don't know," grumbled her husband, not even slowing down.

"Stop the bus, dear," said Mrs. Grizzmeyer, quietly but firmly.

Mr. G. stopped. Mike and Margie tied their bikes to the bus and got on.

"Max," called Mrs. Grizzmeyer. "Take

over the driving. We have to talk. Mike, you sit with your father. I'll sit with Margie."

"It's like a soap opera," said Queenie. "Only it's *real!*" Bonnie shushed her.

"I don't see a wedding ring," said Mrs. Grizzmeyer.

"That's because there was no wedding," said Margie.

"No wedding?" said Mr. Grizzmeyer. "But, but..."

"Easy, Dad," said Mike. "Margie will tell you all about it."

Mike and Margie traded seats. After a deep breath, Margie said, "It was like this. As we biked down the mountain, we were determined to get married. But when we got to the justice of the peace, the whole idea of running away began to worry me. I started thinking maybe we should tell our families first and get married later when they could be present. Now I'm not even sure about that...maybe we aren't even mature enough to get married..."

"Margie, dear," said Mr. Grizzmeyer. "What you just told me proved I was wrong. You *are* mature enough to get married. Have you set a date yet?"

"We were thinking of November," said Margie. "You know, a sort of harvest moon wedding."

The busload of cubs had been listening in complete silence. Now they broke into a loud cheer.

"That'll be enough of that!" snapped Mervyn "Bullhorn" Grizzmeyer. "We've got the All-Camp Games to win. So save your cheering."

Chapter 18
The All-Camp Games—At Last

As the Grizzmeyer bus rolled into Camp Sunshine, it was clear that something big was happening. Buses were pulling into the parking lot. Flags were flying. Groups of campers were marching to and fro.

There were four camps entered in the

All-Camp Games: Camp Sunshine, Camp Blue Mountain, Camp Hilltop, and Camp Grizzmeyer. There were four events: softball, tennis, basketball, and the musical presentation. The All-Camp Games would be scored as follows: four points for a first-place finish, three for a second, two for a third, and one for a fourth. The camp with the most overall points would win the Games.

There was a fanfare from the camp buglers, and the games were under way!

At first it looked like the Grizzmeyer softballers were going to breeze. There was only one problem. Bertha Broom's windmill pitch was so fast that the umpire couldn't see it any better than the batters and called a few walks. One of those walks was on base when a Sunshine batter decided to just close his eyes and swing. He got lucky and connected. The result was an out-of-sight home run, and a 2–1 win for Camp Sunshine.

Camp Grizzmeyer's tennis team also

looked like it was going to breeze—and it
did. The other camps were no match for
Bonnie, Queenie, and two hard-serving
boys from Big Bear City.

Camp Grizzmeyer's basketball team went
into the All-Camp Games with Brother at
point guard, Too-Tall at center, and gang
members Skuzz, Smirk, and Vinnie in sup-
port. They were clearly the most talented
squad in the Games. But one of Too-Tall's
special talents—playing dirty—got him
fouled out in all but one game. The basket-

ball team finished in third place.

After the first three events, Camp Sunshine was in the lead with nine points. Camp Grizzmeyer was second with seven points. The way it was working out, the musical show would make the difference in who won the All-Camp Games—snooty Camp Sunshine or rough-and-ready Camp Grizzmeyer.

The Sunshine theater was jam-packed with campers and counselors from all four camps. Mr. Grizzmeyer's mind was jam-packed—too jam-packed—with thoughts of all the confusing and surprising things that had been happening: Mike and Margie running off to get married, then coming back not married; putting boys and girls on the same teams; putting together a great basketball team and losing. Mr. Grizzmeyer was so deep in thought he hardly noticed that the musical shows were going on.

Until, that is, the Camp Grizzmeyer show started. He knew right away he was going to hate it. It started with Babs Bruno coming on stage holding a sign. The sign said "Camp Quagmire, We Love You! Words and Music by Ferdy Factual and Trudy Brunowitz."

Camp *Quagmire*, thought Mr. Grizzmeyer. Why, those rotten little cubs. Who do they think they are?

A titter from the audience made him that

much angrier. Mr. Brunini, conductor of the Bear Country Orchestra, was all smiles. He was there to judge the musical shows. Mr. Grizzmeyer folded his arms and sat back, ready to hate the show.

But it didn't quite work out that way.

We love you, dear Camp Quagmire,
the place where we are stuck.
We love you, dear Camp Quagmire.
We love your mire and muck.
MUCK
MIRE

There's a lovely lake at Quagmire,
it said in the brochure.
Where, unless you're careful,
you'll catch fish without a lure.
Fish so mean and ugly,
with teeth down to their tails.
But they are not as bad as
those slimy water snails.

We love you, dear Camp Quagmire, a camp just round the bend. We love you, dear Camp Quagmire, but please, please—let this summer end!
It's terrific at Camp Quagmire, you may be very sure. It's super-great and up-to-date, it said in the brochure.
CAMP QUAGMIRE

With insects that could frighten
the monster from Loch Ness.
And consider, please, our mess hall,
it really is a mess!

We love you,
dear Camp Quagmire,
a place of joy and bliss,
where each night
we write our parents,
"I'LL GET YOU FOR THIS!"

Now that our little number
is very nearly done,
we hope you'll understand
our jokes were all in fun.

We've grown to love
Camp Quag-Grizzmeyer.
We hold it very dear.
And so we all are planning
to come back again next year!

P.S., Mr. Grizzmeyer:
Though we're girls and boys,
we're cubs all of a feather.
So we beg you, Mr. Grizzmeyer,
let us get together.

Mr. Grizzmeyer tried his very best to hate the show. But try as he might, he just couldn't. It was so funny, so charming, and at the end so sweet, that he ended up loving it.

So did Mr. Brunini. "Camp Quagmire, We Love You!" came in first, which made Camp Grizzmeyer the overall winner. It was the first time in history that a first-year camp had won the All-Camp Games.

On the ride back to camp, the bus was filled with happy campers, happy counselors, and happy Grizzmeyers. When they arrived, Mr. G. called an all-camp meeting and announced that next summer things would be different. Separate boys' and girls' camps would be a thing of the past.

And that evening, at the big Farewell Dance that marked the end of the camp season, there were no big bands, no country music, and no waltzes. As the whole camp, including Mr. and Mrs. Grizzmeyer, rocked

to the beat of disc jockey Queenie McBear's rock-'n'-roll tapes, everyone knew that Camp Grizzmeyer would never be the same.

We love you, Camp Grizzmeyer

Stan and Jan Berenstain began writing and illustrating books for children in the early 1960s, when their two young sons were beginning to read. That marked the start of the best-selling Berenstain Bears' series. Now, with more than 95 books in print, videos, television shows, and even Berenstain Bears attractions at major amusement parks, it's hard to tell where the Bears end and the Berenstains begin!

Stan and Jan make their home in Bucks County, Pennsylvania, near their sons—Leo, a writer, and Michael, an illustrator—who are helping them with Big Chapter Books stories and pictures. They plan on writing and illustrating many more books for children, especially for their four grandchildren, who keep them well in touch with the kids of today.